The Pir~
Monk

A STORYQUEST BOOK BY
BECCI MURRAY

For Harriet Jeffery,
a StoryQuest Superstar

CHOOSE THE PAGE - UNLOCK THE ADVENTURE

ISBN: 978-1-913944-06-3
Published by Llama House Children's Books

Welcome to your StoryQuest challenge, the book where YOU are in charge of what happens and YOU are the star of the adventure.

Start your quest on the first page, where your challenge will be explained. At the end of each chapter you'll find two options – choose a page to decide what you want to do next.

As a bonus feature, every StoryQuest book has a SPECIAL CHARACTER hidden amongst the pages. Find the character, and they'll give you a STORYQUEST STAR. This will help you unlock the ultimate ending to your adventure.

There are SO many different paths and SO many different endings – some are good, some are bad, some are happy, some are sad. Which will you choose? Will you complete the challenge? And where will your story end?

Good luck, intrepid StoryQuester, and happy reading!

The seaside is lovely at this time of year. You've built a sand-castle, you've eaten an ice-cream the size of your head and you're just taking a quick paddle when two people in a rowing-boat appear on the distant horizon.

"Avast ye!" the man calls out. "Oi'm Jimmy Smallhands and this be me trusty crewmate, One-Eyed Brenda. Be careful in these 'ere waters, matey, for there be *pirates* about."

"Yargh!" cries the enormous woman.

There's a rat on her shoulder. It waves a tiny cutlass and accidentally slices off half of her moustache.

"Erm, okay," you reply. "But I think *you're* the pirates, aren't you?"

Jimmy Smallhands nods.

"Aye, matey, that we are. But we be *good* pirates, see? We be the kind of pirates what feeds yer bones to the fishes then takes our grannies out fer a nice pot o' tea and a slice o' cake."

"Pieces of cake! Pieces of cake!" squawks the rat.

"But if you're pirates," you say, "where's your

1

ship?"

"Alas, matey, the Martha Rose were stolen by a fearsome band of scurvy villains called...*the Pirates of Monkey Island!*"

He shudders when he utters their name, as if someone covered the words in slime and dropped them down the back of his shirt.

You scratch your head with confusion.

"So, what you're saying is...*pirates* stole your pirate ship?"

"Aye, but not just any pirates. *Monkey*-pirates! They pilfered our ship then they thieved our treasure chest too." Jimmy Smallhands sighs heavily. "We were really lookin' forward to eatin' those chocolate coins, weren't we, Brenda?"

"Yargh!"

"You had a treasure chest with *chocolate* coins in it?" you gasp.

"Aye, matey," replies the man, "us pirates can't go a single day without eatin' chocolate, or else we gets the rumbly tummies and that ain't nice fer no-one."

One-Eyed Brenda's stomach grumbles like custard sliding down a plughole. He's right – that wasn't nice for anyone.

"Oh, dear," you reply. "What are you going to do

about it?"

"What're we gunna do?" repeats Jimmy Smallhands. "We're gunna row to Monkey Island and steal it back again, that's what we're gunna do. Trouble is, those scurvy monkey-pirates made the rest of our crew walk the plank and the two of us ain't got no chance of findin' them coins on our own, so…" One-Eyed Brenda picks you up by the arm and plonks you down in the boat. "Welcome aboard, matey!"

"What?!" you cry. "But I can't join your pirate crew!"

"Oi don't see why not," shrugs Jimmy Smallhands.

"Because I'm on holiday," you say. "Because I'm meant to be playing crazy-golf after lunch. Because *I'm not a pirate!*"

"No need to worry about that," smiles the man. "Me and Brenda wouldn't take ye to Monkey Island without the proper piratey equipment. We've got three items to 'elp with yer quest."

"What, like a cannon and a cutlass, or something?"

Jimmy's smile flickers.

"Well, no, but we do 'ave this fine pair of oars. And One-Eyed Brenda's got a telescopic eyeball she can take in and out, so we got that too, ain't we, Brenda?"

"Yargh!"

"But best of all, we got *this.*" Jimmy picks up the rat and drops it onto your lap. It smells of wee. "I mean, it ain't no parrot, but it might just come in useful fer somethin'. So, matey, what do ye say? Will ye come with us to Monkey Island and 'elp steal back our chocolate coins?"

Brenda's eyeball spins full circle then fixes on you like an all-seeing pickled onion.

"Well, all right," you say. "But only if Brenda stops looking at me."

"Swashbucklin'!" cheers Jimmy Smallhands. "And remember, we must find the coins without bein' captured by the monkey-pirates or we'll all be walkin' the plank before sunfall," and with a pull of the oars, you row out across the rolling ocean on a quest to find the stolen treasure.

Your StoryQuest has begun. Turn to page 24 to start your adventure.

"Quick, Brenda," you say, "show Big Baboon Bob your telescopic eyeball!"

The woman skids to a halt. She spins around to face the monkey-pirate, takes hold of her eyeball and pops the thing out of its socket.

PWUCK!

The pupil zooms in and out like a tiny telescope.

WHIR! WHIR! WHIR! WHIR!

Big Baboon Bob stares for a moment in horror, then he squawks like a parrot and runs in the opposite direction.

Swashbucklin'!

"Wow, Brenda, that was great!" you say, as your crewmate shoves her eyeball back into her face. "Let's get to the shipwreck before he comes back."

On the eastern shore of the island, the land is rocky and steep. The huge wreckage of the old vessel looms on the coastline like the washed-up carcass of an ancient sea-monster. Two pieces of its great mast have snapped off and landed in an X shape on what's left of the decking. You'll need to take a closer look if you want to search for the treasure.

5

There are two ways to get up to the deck: you could climb the fallen rigging on the outside of the boat, or go in through a hole in the starboard side.

How will you get up to the mast?

To climb the rigging on the outside of the shipwreck, turn to page 33.

To go in through the hole, turn to page 44.

You decide to use one of the oars to slice through the net, so you take out the item and hack at the rope as if cutting it with a saw.

Hm, that doesn't seem to have worked, so you use the oar like a hammer and whack the rope as if nailing it into a wall. Nope, that hasn't worked either.

Slowly, you raise the oar over your shoulder and strike the net in a karate chop motion.

"Hi-ya!"

But your aim is a little off. The fat end of the wooden paddle slices through the wrong rope and the three of you plummet towards the ground like mammoth acorns, where you land in a prickly hawthorn bush.

A spine gets stuck in One-Eyed Brenda's bottom. You help her limp back to the boat where you carefully remove the thorn, after which you head back to the mainland to recover from the ordeal of seeing Brenda's backside.

Go back to the start of the book to try again, or turn to page 62 to make a different choice.

7

"Yes, please, I'd love to stay for a snack," you reply, and Robinson Cuckoo passes you half of Mr Coconut's head.

"You always did like chicken chow-mein, didn't you, Marjorie?" says the man. You watch in horror as he bites a chunk from the coconut shell and crunches it up like a boiled sweet. "Just wait 'til you see what's for pudding."

The hairy man goes to a small chest in the corner of the room. He opens the lid and an army of crabs crawls out.

He places one of the critters onto the table. You notice a star in one of its claws. There's a picture of your crewmates on one side and the number 16 on the other.

"A StoryQuest Star!" you cheer. "Wow, thank you, Robinson Cuckoo!"

The man wrinkles his nose.

"It's not a star, Marjorie. It's lemon meringue pie." It's not. It's *definitely* a StoryQuest star. "Just memorise the number then hand it over to your crewmates when you've finished your quest to unlock the ultimate end to your story."

"Awesome," you say. "Shall I put it in my pocket for safe-keeping?"

"If you want," shrugs Robinson Cuckoo, "but if I were you, I'd shove it down my trousers like any other sane person. Now, if you'll excuse me, Marjorie, I have a crème brûlée to attend to. Good seeing you again," and the woolly man goes back to his barrel and pulls down the lid.

Congratulations – you've found the StoryQuest Star!
Turn to page 64 to go up to the fallen mast of the shipwreck.

You launch the rat across the jungle. Captain Fluffy-Beard catches it mid-flight and looks curiously down at its whiskery face.

"Shiver me timbers," he gasps, "you're the scariest-lookin' monkey oi ever did see."

"He's not a monkey," you explain, "he's a—"

"Oi knows a monkey when oi sees one," snaps the captain, "and oi'm recruitin' this little lad as the newest member of me monkey-pirate crew. His piratey name shall be Whiskery Pete and if you three bald monkeys don't join too, I shall feed Whiskery Pete to the sharks. Whadda ye say to *that*, me hearties?"

As the person who just threw the rat, you feel responsible for the mess he's in, so you agree to join Captain Fluffy-Beard's crew and are known forever more as Baldy Lobster-Legs of Monkey Island.

Rude.

Go back to the start of the book to try again, or turn to page 40 to make a different choice.

10

You march bravely onto the plank as if walking along a diving board at your local swimming pool and jump elegantly into the cool…

SPLODGE!

Oh, dear.

The tide is out at this time of day, so instead of landing in water, you've splatted into the muddy sand of the eastern coast. It takes five hours to dig yourself free, by which time the Howler Twins have captured your crewmates and eaten all of the chocolate coins for themselves.

Go back to the start of the book to try again, or turn to page 83 to make a different choice.

One-Eyed Brenda walks bravely towards the plank.

"Time to swim with the fishes, ye scabby codfish!" cries the first Howler Twin.

"Yer a cabby codfish!" laughs the other. "Yo, ho, ho, ho, hooo!"

Brenda's eyeball zooms in on a tiny crack in the ship's deck.

WHIR! WHIR! WHIR! WHIR!

The huge woman places her feet on the crack, and jumps.

SMASH!

The ship is so rotten that the floor gives way and the whole group of you tumble down through the wreckage as the old vessel splits in two.

Five pairs of feet hammer into the muddy sand beneath the boat like darts in a corkboard.

SPLODGE!

SPLODGE!

SPLODGE!

SPLODGE!

SPLODGE!

It's a bit of a result for One-Eyed Brenda – she doesn't have to walk the plank after all. But it also means you'll be stuck here until the tide comes in and washes you out of the sand, by which time the other monkey-pirates will have realised you're here and scoffed the chocolate coins for themselves.

Go back to the start of the book to try again, or turn to page 64 to make a different choice.

13

You climb down from the wreckage and onto the shore.

"Brenda," you say, "as there aren't any coins on the shipwreck, would you mind using your telescopic eyeball to search for another X?"

"Yargh!" replies One-Eyed Brenda.

A gentle whirring sound comes from inside the woman's head, as her eyeball spins in its socket.

WHIR! WHIR! WHIR! WHIR!

The pupil pops out like a tiny ice-cream cone.

POP!

And zooms in on the other side of the island with a rusty, *CREEEEEEEEAK!* It's the most disgusting thing you've ever seen or heard in your life, but it's also pretty awesome.

The woman points to the south of the island.

"Brenda says there be another X on top o' Big Face Rock," explains Jimmy Smallhands. "But Big Face Rock is difficult to climb and dangerous too."

Brenda points to the west of the island.

"She says there also be an X in the window of an ancient ruin," says Jimmy, "but an evil spirit guards the buildin' and chases away anyone who goes near it. I gotta tell ye, matey, I don't much fancy visitin' *either* place, but oi'll leave the choice up to ye."

Which X would you like to look at next?

An evil spirit? No, thanks! I'll go to Big Face Rock. Turn to page 31.
An evil spirit? Cool! I'll go to the ancient ruin. Turn to page 78.

"Shiver me timbers!" cries Jimmy Smallhands. "Ye found the StoryQuest Star! Time fer a treat, matey."

With a small wink, he hurls the star into the ocean. It hits a wave and the sea turns to gold, as an enormous ship *made of chocolate* rises up from the blue.

"That's the tastiest ship I've ever seen!" you gasp.

"And it be *your* ship," smiles Jimmy. "Ye can sail the seven seas in this beauty. Ain't that right, Brenda?"

The woman's eyeball zooms in on the humungous lump of floating chocolate.

"Y…y…y…" she stammers. But the word doesn't want to come out. "Y…y…y…*you should just eat it!*"

One-Eyed Brenda's cheeks turn pink.

"I think that's a brilliant idea, Brenda," you laugh. "But that's a lot of chocolate for one person. Does anyone want to help me finish it off?"

And Brenda replies, "Yargh!"

Congratulations, you've finished your quest and found the ultimate end to your adventure. You're a StoryQuest legend, matey. Swashbucklin'!

Untying the knots is almost impossible. Captain Fluffy-Beard has pulled them so tight with his tiny hands, you can't get a grip on the string.

"This be a job fer someone with bloomin' small fingers," smiles Jimmy Smallhands, and in a blur of tattoos, he unravels the string until a big hole appears in the net. Swashbucklin'!

One by one, you crawl through the hole and sit on the nearest branch. Captain Fluffy-Beard said the chocolate treasure isn't buried in the jungle, so you scan the area for other places to search.

To the north of the island, there's a small lagoon with a large X hovering over the pool. Or there's a battered shipwreck to the east, with a broken mast that has fallen in the shape of an X.

Where would you like to go next, me hearty?

Let's visit the shipwreck. Turn to page 82.
Let's go to the lagoon. Turn to page 53.

17

You leave the shark-infested waters and head towards the shipwreck on the eastern coast of the island, where the land is rocky and steep. The huge wreckage of the old vessel looms on the coastline like the washed-up carcass of an ancient sea-monster.

Two pieces of its great mast have snapped off and landed in an X shape on what's left of the decking. You'll need to take a closer look if you want to search for the treasure.

There are two ways to get up to the deck: you could climb the fallen rigging on the outside of the boat, or go in through a hole in the starboard side.

How will you get up to the mast?

To climb the rigging on the outside of the shipwreck, turn to page 33.

To go in through the hole, turn to page 44.

18

You lie on your stomach and reach out to One-Eyed Brenda with the oar. She grabs hold and clutches it tightly, as you pull her out of the sand.

"Think yer clever, do ye?" growls Stinky Silverback Shelly. "We'll soon see about that. 'Ave a whiff of these bad-boys, me hearties."

The gorilla raises her arms and a terrible pong wafts over the beach. It hits your face like a wave, stinging your eyes and clouding your brain, until your eyes roll back in your head and you pass-out on the sand.

Crumbs! You've been thwarted by the smell of Stinky Silverback Shelly's armpits and your quest has come to a rather stinky end. But you rescued your crewmate and for that you are a truly magnificent human.

Swashbucklin'!

Go back to the start of the book to try again, or turn to page 35 to make a different choice.

19

You climb up to the crow's nest for a better look at the island. The view from here is fantastic. You can literally see right across to the other side of the—

SNAP!

Uh oh. The pole holding the crow's nest must have been damaged when the ship crashed and the extra weight has snapped it in two. You plummet towards the deck like a falling anchor, crash through the rotten wood and drop into the ship's galley.

You land next to a very hairy man.

He's carving a face into a coconut.

"How good of you to drop in on us," he says. "Oh dear, you seem to have hurt yourself. Have a drink out of Mr Coconut's head. It'll make you feel much better."

But drinking out of Mr Coconut's head doesn't make you feel better, so your crewmates wrap you up in bandages like an Egyptian mummy and send you back to the mainland to recover.

Go back to the start of the book to try again, or turn to page 47 to make a different choice.

You start the long climb to the top of Big Face Rock, pulling yourself onto the chin, over the bottom lip and up towards the biggest nose you've ever seen in your life.

The tip of the nose is round and smooth. It's going to be tricky to hold on if you try to climb over it, but there's a dim light shining out through the rock's left nostril. It could be a secret tunnel leading up to the peak.

Will you climb over the nose to reach the summit, or do you want to crawl up the nostril?

I want to crawl up the nostril, please. Turn to page 74.
No-one *wants* to crawl up a nostril. I'll climb over the nose please. Turn to page 51.

Making a shark costume is easy. You take some palm tree leaves and sew them together with long lengths of grass, then you whittle a set of teeth from a coconut and – *hey presto!* – you have yourself a cunning disguise.

As you enter the lagoon, the shark's head rises up out of the water.

"Why, hello," grins the giant fish. "Welcome to the Monkey Island lagoon. We don't get many giant slugs around here."

"I'm not a slug," you reply. "I'm a shark like you. See? I've got the teeth and everything."

"My dear," says the shark, "ten out of ten for effort, but you most definitely do *not* have the teeth."

She flashes you her razor-sharp set of gnashers. She's right. Your teeth are rubbish compared to hers.

"Okay, so, I'm not a shark," you say, your voice trembling. "But I made this costume because I want to search the lagoon. You see, I'm on a quest to find some missing chocolate coins and I think they might be under this X."

"There's no chocolate in here," says the shark. "If

there was chocolate in my lagoon, I'd be eating it right now, because I'm absolutely *starving*."

The shark moves towards you and her jaws open, but a big hook drops suddenly into the water. It catches hold of your palm-leaf fin and lifts you out of the pool.

As the shark sinks miserably into the shadowy water, you look up to see a hideous monkey face staring down at you. Crikey, it's Big Baboon Bob! He's one of Captain Fluffy-Beard's crew!

How are you going to escape?

I'll keep pretending I'm a shark and scare him away.
Turn to page 46.
I'll bite through the fishing-line with my coconut teeth and scarper. Turn to page 81.

You row out across the shimmering ocean until a small island appears on the distant horizon.

"That be Monkey Island," says Jimmy Smallhands, as your rowing-boat enters a crescent-shaped cove. "If we wants to find the missin' coins, we'll 'ave to look fer where X marks the spot."

You hide the boat in a patch of long grass and scan the white beach. Someone has made a big X out of seaweed on the sand.

But beyond the cove, a palm tree jungle looms in the distance like an angry storm cloud. Two of the trunks are taller than the others and they've crossed over to form an enormous X in the sky.

Where would you like to look first, StoryQuester?

I'll check out the X on the beach please. Turn to page 35.

I'd like to go to the palm tree jungle. Turn to page 42.

Leading your crew to safety, you push past the monkey-pirates and run out of the ancient ruin. Captain Fluffy-Beard chortles as he runs upstairs and holds up a chest full of chocolate coins to the X-shaped window.

"Is *this* what ye were lookin' for?" grins the captain. He unwraps one of the delicious coins and shoves it into his pretty little face. "Well, we're gunna eat the whole bloomin' lot and you'll all have rumbly tummies fer the rest of yer lives," and his motley crew laugh hysterically.

You look sadly down at your feet as the sun lowers in the evening sky. It casts an orange glow over the island, silhouetting the ancient ruins against the reddening horizon. Sunlight pours through the upstairs window of the roof-less building. It casts the shadow of an X onto the ground in front of you.

Your heart races.

"X marks the spot," you gasp, hardly able to believe your eyes. "Quick, Jimmy Smallhands, pass me one of those oars."

Hurriedly, you dig down into the soft ground until

the tip of the oar hits the lid of a wooden chest and with trembling hands you open it. A hundred or more golden chocolate bars are glistening in the fading sunlight. Crikey! This treasure must have been buried here by another pirate crew!

One of the Howler Twins appears in the doorway of the ruin.

"Captain!" he yells. "They be findin' buried chocolate bars, Captain, and they're much bigger than our coins! Come quick, come quick!"

Okay, StoryQuester, this could be your final choice – will you take your loot and run away from the monkey-pirate crew, or will you tell those nasty bullies exactly what you think of them?

I'll tell the nasty bullies exactly what I think of them. Turn to page 66.

Let's grab the treasure chest and leg it! Turn to page 37.

You gulp down the water and put the shell back on the table. At once, a grubby-looking man with torn clothes and more hair than a yak bursts out of an old barrel.

"Marjorie!" he warbles, as if all his Christmases have just come at once. "I've poured that water every day for fifty years, Marjorie, in the hope you'll pop over for dinner." He pulls a silver tray from behind his back. It has a live sea-snail on it. "Amuse-bouche?"

You eye the snail and the snail eyes you.

"Erm, no, thank you," you reply. "Sorry, but…do I know you?"

"Oh, Marjorie, you're such a card. It's me! Robinson Cuckoo! I've waited half a century for you to arrive, Marjorie, with no-one to talk to except Mr Coconut over there. It's a wonder I haven't completely lost my marbles." He pulls a jelly-fish out of his trousers. "Strawberry trifle?"

Robinson Cuckoo washed up on Monkey Island when his ship crashed into the rocks. You'd feel mean telling him you're not Marjorie, so instead you play along and apologise for your late arrival.

"Sorry to keep your waiting, Robinson," you say, "but I'm afraid I can't stay for dinner right now. You see, I'm on a quest to find some missing coins."

The man looks sadly over at the empty dinner table. He puts the jellyfish on his head and sighs.

"I understand, Marjorie," he says, miserably. "But can't you stay for just one little snack? I really have been ever so lonely."

He rips the coconut man's head off his driftwood shoulders, smashes it open on the table and offers you the biggest half. Do you want to share Mr Coconut's head with Robinson Cuckoo, or will you make an excuse and go up to the deck?

This guy's a nutjob. I'll make an excuse and go up to the deck. Turn to page 64.

I'd love to eat Mr Coconut's head! Turn to page 8.

You find a strand of seaweed from the shoreline and throw one end of it to Brenda. The woman grabs hold. She clings on tightly as you and Jimmy pull with all of your might, and—

SNAP!

The seaweed breaks.

Brenda sinks further into the ground and with a muffled, "Yargh!" she completely disappears.

"Har, har, har!" laughs Stinky Silverback Shelly. "That were more fun than firin' cannonballs at dolphins."

You hear footsteps coming from underneath the quicksand. It sounds like One-Eyed Brenda has landed in some kind of secret chamber. Will you try to find her or head towards the palm tree jungle to continue your quest?

Leave my crewmate behind? No way! Let's try to find her. Turn to page 88.

I'll go to the palm tree jungle and continue my quest. Turn to page 40.

"Quick, run for the stairs!" you call out to your crew, and you dash up the dusty old steps.

Below the X of the broken window frame, there's a treasure chest. Brenda's stomach gurgles at the sight of it.

"There be our chocolate coins!" cries Jimmy. "There be our scrummy treasure!"

Captain Fluffy-Beard and his crew appear at the top of the stairs.

"Think yer real smart, don't ye?" he snarls. "But tell me, ye scurvy scoundrels, how do ye plan to get past *us* with your loot?"

The monkey-pirates have you cornered. They tie you up and chomp down every last one of the coins, then they send you back to the mainland with nothing more than a chest full of wrappers.

That's a rum deal when you're so close to finishing your quest. Make another choice to complete your challenge.

Go back to the start of the book to try again, or turn to page 85 to make a different choice.

Big Face Rock is a big rock that looks like a face and it was named by someone with no imagination.

Two enormous boulders stare down over a craggy nose as you gaze up at the X on the very top of the rock's head. Someone will have to go up there to look for the chocolate coins.

"Brenda," you say, "would you mind climbing to the summit of Big Face Rock to look for the treasure?"

One-Eyed Brenda curls up in a ball on the ground and quivers with fear. You take that as a, no. It looks like either you or Jimmy Smallhands will have to make the treacherous climb instead.

Yes, please, I'd love to climb Big Face Rock. Turn to page 21.

No, thanks, I'll let Jimmy climb it. Turn to page 49.

"Jump for the creeper!" you call out to your crewmates.

The other end of the plant is attached to a wooden beam on the ceiling and the old roof creaks as the three of you shimmy up to the rafters.

"You're going to break that," says the little monkey ghost, matter-of-factly. "If you break that ceiling, I'll be really cross with you."

A huge crack snakes across the beam. It won't hold you up for much longer. You'll have to lighten the load so the roof doesn't collapse, but how?

I'll let go of the creeper to lighten the load and face the little monkey ghost myself. That sounds like the brave thing to do. Turn to page 72.

Let's drop the rat. Turn to page 85.

The rigging looks fairy sturdy, so Jimmy and Brenda keep look-out from the shore as you haul yourself up to the deck.

The old wreckage is creaky and damp, its sails are tattered and torn, the crow's nest has actual crows in it and the cannons are covered in barnacles.

You walk towards the broken mast to investigate the X. There's an old rum barrel directly below the cross, but you search inside it to find nothing more than seasnails and crabs. There's not a single chocolate coin to be seen on the whole ship.

Turning to leave, you see two identical monkey-pirates standing behind you. It's the Howler Twins, Captain Fluffy-Beard's first and second mates.

"What're ye doin' on our shipwreck, ye mangy varmint?" snarls the first twin.

"Yer a mangy varmint!" laughs the second. "Yo, ho, ho, ho, hooo!"

You try to think of a convincing answer to the monkey-pirate's question. But you can't think of one, so instead you reply, "I'm delivering pizzas."

You're not sure why you said that.

"You can't deliver pizzas 'ere," says the first Howler Twin. "It's only monkey-pirates what are allowed on Monkey Island, ye hornswaggling barrel-bellied blighter."

"Yer a hornswaggling barrel-bellied blighter!" laughs the second. "Yo, ho, ho, ho, hooo!"

"And if ye ain't a monkey-pirate, you'll 'ave to walk the plank, ye filthy parrot-faced rapscallion."

"Yer a filthy parrot-faced rapscallion! Yo, ho, ho, ho, hooo!" The second twin lowers his furry eyebrows. "What's a pizza?"

How are you going to escape from the Howler Twins?

To tell them you're a monkey-pirate, turn to page 47.

To walk the plank then swim back to shore, turn to page 87.

The closer you get to the seaweed X, the deeper your feet sink into the ground. You stop to investigate the muddy sand.

"I don't be likin' the look of this," says Jimmy Smallhands. "I reckons that X be a trick. I reckons we be headin' for quicksand."

The two of you hurry to the side of the beach, but One-Eyed Brenda has already gone on ahead. She sinks into the sand like a stone through jelly, until only the top half of her body is sticking up out of the ground.

Suddenly, from the other side of the X, a gorilla appears. She's wearing a red bandana and beating her chest like a drum.

It's Stinky Silverback Shelly, one of the monkey-pirate crew!

"Captain Fluffy-Beard said you'd come lookin' fer those chocolate coins we pilfered," snarls the gorilla. "That's why oi made that seaweed X on the beach, to trick ye onto the quicksand. You'll never find where we've *really* hidden the treasure, ye motley scallywags."

Oh, no! One-Eyed Brenda has fallen for Stinky

Silverback Shelly's trick and she's sinking fast. You can't walk on the quicksand to pull her out, so you'll have to use an item to reach her.

You could try using one of the oars, or grab a string of seaweed from the shoreline. Which item do you think will work best?

Let's use one of the oars. Turn to page 19.

I'll try using a strand of seaweed. Turn to page 29.

The three of you take hold of the chest full of chocolate bars. Wowsers, it's really heavy! Jimmy Smallhands clutches his back and drops his side of the box.

"Me back! Me back!" he cries, holding your arm to keep himself upright. "I've only gone and put me back out!"

The treasure chest lands on One-Eyed Brenda's foot.

"*YAAAAAARGH!*"

With your crewmates injured, you lift the chest on your own. But it's too heavy for you to run with and the monkey-pirates are soon snatching it out of your hands.

You were so close to completing your challenge, matey, but it looks like you'll have to stand up to those mean monkeys if you want to finish your quest.

Go back to the start of the book to try again, or turn to page 25 to make a different choice.

You launch the rat across the jungle. Captain Fluffy-Beard catches it mid-flight and looks curiously down at its whiskery face.

"Shiver me timbers," he gasps, "you're the scariest-lookin' monkey oi ever did see."

"He's not a monkey," you explain, "he's a—"

"Oi knows a monkey when oi sees one," snaps the captain, "and oi'm recruitin' this little lad as the newest member of me monkey-pirate crew. His piratey name shall be Whiskery Pete and if you three bald monkeys don't join too, I shall feed Whiskery Pete to the sharks. Whadda ye say to *that*, me hearties?"

As the person who just threw the rat, you feel responsible for the mess he's in, so you join Captain Fluffy-Beard's crew and are known forever more as Baldy Lobster-Legs of Monkey Island.

Rude.

Go back to the start of the book to try again, or turn to page 42 to make a different choice.

"I'd love to do some yoga with you," you say to the golden eagle.

After trying out a few poses, you sit next to the great bird and meditate as the sun melts into the distant horizon.

"Relaxing, isn't it?" he says.

"It really is," you reply. "In fact, I feel as if I could almost…fall…ZZZZZZZZ!"

Oh, dear. You've fallen asleep on the summit of Big Face Rock and you don't wake up until the monkey-pirates have stuffed every last one of the chocolate coins into their furry little mouths.

Go back to the start of the book to try again, or turn to page 51 to make a different choice.

The palm tree jungle is alive with the sound of tropical birds and animals. As you pick your way through the undergrowth, a little face pops out from the foliage. It's *so* fluffy and cute! Its cheeks are like two tiny pom-poms, its nose is no bigger than a button and its sparkling blue eyes are glistening like the ocean itself.

"Hello, there, little guy," you say to the adorable creature. "Aren't you a sweet little—"

The face leaps out of the bush, grabs hold of you by the collar and pins you to the ground.

"Scurvy parrot-faced rapscallion!" snarls the creature. The animal's delicate eyelashes flutter like two butterflies. "What're ye doin' on my island, ye mangy son of a sea-dog?"

Jimmy Smallhands starts quivering like a jellyfish.

"It's Captain Fluffy-Beard," he stammers. "He's the leader of the monkey-pirates and the cutest villain to ever 'ave lived."

Captain Fluffy-Beard wants to know what you're doing on his island. You can't tell him you're here to steal back the treasure or he'll pummel you with his

40

sweet little fists.

What are you going to say?

I'll say we're on a banana hunt. Turn to page 69.
I'm saying nothing. Let's set the rat on him! Turn to
page 10.

The palm tree jungle is alive with the sound of tropical birds and animals. As you pick your way through the undergrowth, a little face pops out from the foliage. It's *so* fluffy and cute! Its cheeks are like two tiny pom-poms, its nose is no bigger than a button and its sparkling blue eyes are glistening like the ocean itself.

"Hello, there, little guy," you say to the adorable creature. "Aren't you a sweet little—"

The face leaps out of the bush, grabs hold of you by the collar and pins you to the ground.

"Scurvy parrot-faced rapscallion!" snarls the creature. The animal's delicate eyelashes flutter like two butterflies. "What're ye doin' on my island, ye mangy son of a sea-dog?"

Jimmy Smallhands starts quivering like a jellyfish.

"It's Captain Fluffy-Beard," he stammers. "He's the leader of the monkey-pirates and the cutest villain who ever lived."

Captain Fluffy-Beard wants to know what you're doing on his island. You can't tell him you're here to steal back the treasure or he'll pummel you with his sweet little fists.

What are you going to say?

I'll say we're on a banana hunt. Turn to page 62.

I'm saying nothing. Let's set the rat on him! Turn to page 38.

The hole in the starboard side of the shipwreck is big enough for *you* but much too small for One-Eyed Brenda's bottom. Watching her try to squeeze through it is like watching someone trying to push a bouncy-castle through a drainpipe.

"Oi reckons me and Brenda should stay out 'ere on the shore," says Jimmy Smallhands. "We can keep a look-out and if we sees any monkey-pirates, we'll make a noise like a dolphin to let ye know. Ain't that right, Brenda?"

"Yargh!"

Thanking your crewmates, you climb through the hole. The inside of the wreckage smells damp and rotten. Sea crustaceans cling to the walls, crabs scuttle in and out of the woodwork, and the floor is slick with a carpet of green algae.

At the centre of the room, you see a table. Six plates have been laid out in front of the chairs and the silver cutlery has been polished until you can see your reflection in it. That's strange. Why are the knives and forks so shiny? And why do you feel like you're being watched?

You turn suddenly to see a man with a coconut head, driftwood arms and a body made out of stuffed palm-tree leaves at the far end of the table. He's been carefully tied together with plaited grass and a creepy smile has been carved into his face. Perhaps the monkey-pirates made him to scare you away from the treasure.

The fake man has a shell of fresh water on the table in front him. Searching for treasure is thirsty work and you'd like to take a sip, but you really should be getting on with your quest. Will you drink the water, or go upstairs to investigate the X?

I'll take a drink of water please. Turn to page 27.
I'll leave the water where it is and go up to the deck.
Turn to page 83.

"Rargh!" you say, showing the monkey-pirate your fine set of coconut teeth. "I'm a shark! Rargh, rargh!"

"Bloomin' barnacles!" cries Big Baboon Bob. "Oi've only gone and caught meself a tasty snack. Captain Fluffy-Beard loves a shark-meat sandwich. Just ye wait 'til he sees what oi got fer our supper."

You try to tell Big Baboon Bob you're not really a shark, but he's not listening – he's too busy putting you on the menu for tonight's monkey-pirate feast and covering you with garlic.

I guess your shark impression was just too bloomin' good. Rargh!

Go back to the start of the book to try again, or turn to page 22 to make a different choice.

"Ahoy, thar, me hearties!" you cry, in your best piratey voice. The Howler Twins look at each other with confusion. "Ye can't be makin' me walk the plank, for I be a monkey-pirate too, see? Splice the mainbrace! Man overboard! Shiver me timbers! Pieces of eight! Heave ho and walk the plank! Yo, ho, ho, ho, hooo!"

As monkey-pirate impressions go, it's not bad.

"Oh," says the first twin, scratching his furry head. "Why didn't ye say so? Oi suppose if ye be a monkey-pirate too, we'd better be lettin' ye go or Captain Fluffy-Beard will be terribly cross."

"Thanks very much," you reply. "I mean...too right, ye hornbucklin' swoggly-doggly sea-cucumbers!" and with a shrug of their shoulders, the Howler Twins leave the shipwreck.

Swashbucklin'!

You didn't find any treasure on the wreckage, so you'll need to search somewhere else for the coins. But there are no more Xs in sight. You could climb up to the crow's nest for a better view of the island, or leave the shipwreck and ask Brenda to use her telescopic eyeball for a good look around.

Which will it be, matey?

I'd like to climb up to the crow's nest. Turn to page 20.
I'll leave the shipwreck and ask Brenda to use her
telescopic eyeball. Turn to page 89.

Jimmy Smallhands starts the long and dangerous climb to the top of Big Face Rock. He pulls himself over the chin, onto the bottom lip and finally climbs up to the stony moustache for a quick rest below the enormous nostrils.

"Is everything all right, Jimmy?" you call out.

"There ain't no way to get around the nose!" he replies. "Oi'm gunna 'ave to climb over it!"

"You can do it, Jimmy!" you shout. "We believe in you! Just go for it!"

"Yargh!" adds One-Eyed Brenda.

The rock's nose looks like a humungous turnip. Jimmy reaches for the end of it, but his hands are too small to hold on. His foot slips and he bounces down the side of Big Face Rock like a rubber ball, twisting his ankle and grazing his knee.

You and Brenda feel guilty for having encouraged your crewmate, so you take him back to the mainland for a doctor to bandage his leg. The treasure will have to wait for another day, but you're an awesome friend and that's much more important than any amount of chocolate.

49

Swashbucklin'!

Go back to the start of the book to try again, or turn to page 31 to make a different choice.

Your hands are just big enough to take hold of the huge nose and heave yourself onto the bridge. But the rock here is slippery and smooth. Your feet slide over the surface like ice – you're going nowhere fast.

Suddenly, the rocks starts to twitch. You're tickling it with your feet and the itching is too much to bear.

Big Face Rock wrinkles its nose as it tries to hold on to a sneeze. The creases make a ladder rising up to the peak. You place a foot into the bottommost wrinkle and scramble up to the summit.

There's the X! It's big, it's X-shaped and…it has *feathers,* for some reason.

"Namaste," says the feathery shape.

You frown. It isn't an X at all. It's a golden eagle, standing perfectly still with its legs apart and its wings held up in the air.

"Hello," you say. "I thought you were an X. I don't mean to be rude, but what are you doing?"

"Yoga," replies the eagle. "This, my friend, is what we yogis call a warrior pose. You should try it. It's very calming."

Would you like to do some yoga with the golden eagle, or get on with your quest?

I love yoga – let's do it! Turn to page 39.
This is a StoryQuest not a yoga retreat. I'd like to get on with my quest. Turn to page 58.

The lagoon is a small circle of still water with a faint smell of eggs. The X you saw is made out of two wooden bridges that cross over at the centre of the pool.

"If the chocolate coins be hidden 'ere," says Jimmy Smallhands, "they must be down there in the water."

"Yargh!" agrees One-Eyed Brenda.

A dark shape catches your eye from below the surface and a triangular fin slices through the murky water. It cuts across the pool like a knife as the head of a shark rises up from the pool.

Eek! These are *shark-infested* waters! And if the treasure's hidden beneath the bridges, you'll have to jump in.

Do you have a cunning plan to fool the sharks, or would you like to change your mind and investigate the shipwreck instead?

I have a cunning plan – I'll make myself a shark costume before I jump in. Turn to page 22.

That's not a cunning plan. I'll go to the shipwreck instead. Turn to page 18.

"I'd like Jimmy Smallhands to go first," you tell the Howler Twins, "because he looks like he'll float better than One-Eyed Brenda. No offence, Brenda."

"Yargh," shrugs the woman.

"Oi will be honoured to face the plank first, matey," replies Jimmy with a wink, and the monkey-pirates march him across the deck with his hands tied firmly behind his back.

You're surprised at how keen Jimmy Smallhands is to meet his watery fate. But then you notice his fingers are wriggling around and before you know what's happening his tiny hands slip free of the rope. He grabs the two terrible monkey-pirates by the tails and they yelp as he slings the pair of them over the side of the shipwreck and into the muddy sand below.

SPLODGE!

Swashbucklin'!

"I do be reckonin' that were your fault, ye mangy barnacle-brain," says the first twin to his brother.

"Oi'm a mangy barnacle-brain!" laughs the second. "Yo, ho— Hey, who are ye callin' a barnacle-brain, ye bloomin' tentacle-head?"

You untie One-Eyed Brenda and gather your crew near the X.

"I've looked all over this ship for the chocolate coins," you tell them, "but there's nothing here. We'd better find another X to investigate and fast, before the Howler Twins escape from that mud and cause any more trouble."

How would you like to search the island for more Xs?

I'll climb up to the crow's nest for a better view of the island. Turn to page 80.

I'll leave the shipwreck and ask Brenda to use her telescopic eyeball to search the island. Turn to page 14.

"Not to worry, matey," says Jimmy Smallhands. "You've finished yer quest and that's all that matters. And as a thank you fer all yer hard work, me and Brenda 'ave got a little surprise fer ye."

One-Eyed Brenda takes a mountain of gold chocolate bars out of the treasure chest and places them into your arms.

"Wow!" you gasp. "Is this all for *me?*"

"Aye," replies Jimmy, "it be your share of the treasure and oi reckons you've earned it. That there is a lot o' chocolate though, so make sure ye don't eat it before supper or it'll spoil yer appetite. Ain't that right, Brenda?"

The woman's eyeball zooms in on the heap of chocolate. Her mouth starts to water.

"Y…y…y…" she stammers. But the word doesn't want to come out. "Y…y…y…*you should eat it right now!*"

One-Eyed Brenda slams a hand over her own mouth and her cheeks turn pink.

"Thanks, Brenda," you laugh. "Do you really think that's a good idea though?"

And Brenda replies, "Yargh!"

Congratulations! You've completed your quest and you're a pirating StoryQuest hero. Swashbucklin'!

If you'd like to read more StoryQuest adventures, take a look in the back of this book.

"Thanks for the invite," you say to the golden eagle, "but I don't have time for yoga. You see, I'm on a quest to find some missing chocolate coins. I don't suppose you've seen any lying around up here?"

"I'm afraid not," says the bird. "But I was performing a downward dog this morning when I noticed a group of monkeys going into the ancient ruin with an old treasure chest. You might want to try there."

Thanking the eagle, you climb down to your crewmates and before long the three of you are standing in front of the ancient ruin. Above the doorway, there's a rotten window-frame. It forms a perfect X at the top of the building, so you step inside and head for a dusty staircase in the back wall.

One-Eyed Brenda stops in her tracks. She points a trembling finger over your shoulder and you turn to see a pale figure floating behind you.

Blimey, it's the evil spirit!

Except, it's not evil at all. It's a little monkey ghost with a cross look on her face.

"What're you doing in my ruin?" demands the

58

ghost. "Get out before I scare you away with my ghostly woo-ing."

GULP.

You'd really like to leave now, but you'd also like to search upstairs for the treasure. What are you going to do?

There's a creeper hanging down from the ceiling. Let's jump for it and climb away from the little monkey ghost. Turn to page 32.

I did enough climbing on Big Face Rock. Let's throw the rat at her. Turn to page 76.

You stop running and turn suddenly.

"Oh look, there's a bear!" you shout, pointing over Big Baboon Bob's shoulder.

Your acting skills are magnificent and the monkey-pirate panics. He spins full circle, waving his arms as if being chased by a wasp, before running away with his tail between his legs.

Swashbucklin'!

But suddenly you realise Jimmy Smallhands and One-Eyed Brenda are also vanishing into the distance. You forgot to explain your plan to them and you're such a talented actor they believed what you said about the bear, so they're running away as fast as their legs will carry them.

By the time you catch up with them, Big Baboon Bob has convinced the other monkey-pirates to set sail for a safer island and they've taken the chocolate coins with them. Drat that imaginary bear!

Go back to the start of the book to try again, or turn to page 81 to make a different choice.

"Quickly, run for the stairs!" you call out to your crew, and you dash up the dusty old steps.

Below the X of the broken window frame, there's a treasure chest. Brenda's stomach gurgles at the sight of it.

"There be our chocolate coins!" cries Jimmy. "There be our scrummy treasure!"

Captain Fluffy-Beard and his crew appear at the top of the stairs.

"Think yer real smart, don't ye?" he snarls. "But tell me, ye scurvy scoundrels, how do ye plan to get past *us* with your loot?"

The monkey-pirates have you cornered. They tie you up and chomp down every last one of the coins, then they send you back to the mainland with nothing more than a chest full of wrappers.

That's a rum deal when you're so close to finishing your quest. Make another choice to complete your challenge.

Go back to the start of the book to try again, or turn to page 76 to make a different choice.

"We're on a banana hunt," you tell Captain Fluffy-Beard. "Yep, we're just three banana-hunters and a rat out looking for some tasty yellow snacks. There are loads of them at the top of these two crossed-over trees, so if you don't mind, we'll just climb up and take a look."

The monkey-pirate narrows his eyes.

"Not so fast, landlubber," he says. "Oi'm a *monkey.* Don't you reckon oi'd know if there were bananas on this island?" He has a point. "And if you ain't 'ere for the fruit, I reckons you've come to steal me treasure."

Captain Fluffy-Beard wraps his tail around a small branch and pulls. The leaves on the ground shoot into the air as a big net scoops you up. It lifts you to the top of the tree, where you dangle helplessly with your crew like a rather strange-looking coconut.

The monkey-pirate captain howls with laughter.

"The chocolate coins ain't hidden in the jungle," he hoots, "and yer'll never find the right X by *hangin' around* in a tree all day. Oi'll let ye down in a week or two though…if you're lucky," and he scampers away through the trees with his little tail floating behind him like a pretty feather.

Oo, you'd like to boot that sweet little ball of fluffiness to the other side of the island. But first things first – how are you going to free your crew from this net?

I'll use an oar to slice through the string. Turn to page 7.

Let's untie the knots to open it up. Turn to page 17.

Leaving the galley, you climb up the small wooden staircase and step out onto the ship's deck. The sails are tattered and torn, the crow's nest has actual crows in it and the cannons are covered in barnacles. There's an old rum barrel directly below the X of the broken mast, but you search inside to find nothing more than seasnails and crabs.

There's not a single chocolate coin to be found on this whole bloomin' ship!

"Welcome aboard, ye scurvy stowaway," snarls a voice from behind you.

"Yer a scurvy stowaway! Yo, ho, ho, ho, hooo!" laughs another.

You turn to see two identical monkey-pirates standing behind you. Jimmy Smallhands and One-Eyed Brenda are with them and their hands have been tied up with rope.

Cripes! It's the Howler Twins – Captain Fluffy-Beard's first and second mates!

"We've captured yer crew and taken 'em hostage, the mangy sea-dogs," says the first monkey.

"They be mangy sea-dogs!" laughs the second

twin. "Yo, ho, ho, ho, hooo!"

"We're gunna make 'em walk the plank," says the first, pointing to a wooden board nailed to the side of the wreckage, "and *you're* gunna choose which one of 'em goes first, ye fish-faced hornswaggler."

"Yer a fish-faced hornswaggler! Yo, ho, ho, ho, hooo!"

Well, this is terrible. Not only do you have to decide which crew member will walk the plank first, but that monkey-pirate's laugh is *really annoying*.

Who will you choose to take the plunge first, matey?

I'll choose Jimmy Smallhands. Turn to page 54.

I'll choose One-Eyed Brenda. Turn to page 12.

You place both hands on your hips and peer down at the tiny monkey-pirate captain. He reminds you of a teddy-bear you used to have.

"Stop being so *mean!*" you tell him. The captain looks a bit confused. No-one has ever stood-up to him before. "*We* found this treasure, not *you*. What would your mothers say if they found out how horrible you are to your fellow pirates?"

Big Baboon Bob looks sheepishly down at his feet.

"She'd send me to bed with a good tellin'-off," he replies, "and she'd stop me pocket money for a month."

The Howler Twins chew at their bottom lips and their cheeks glow redder than Big Baboon Bob's bottom.

"Our mammy would say we've been very naughty monkeys," says the first twin, "because we ain't supposed to eat chocolate before supper."

"And we ain't allowed to cross the ocean on our own yet neither," adds the second.

You turn to Captain Fluffy-Beard and look him square in the eye.

"And what about you, Captain? What would *your* mother say if she knew about all the terrible things you've been up to?"

The captain folds his tiny arms and pouts.

"She'd say if oi steals any more chocolate, she'll send me parrot back to the pet-shop and lock me cannonballs in a cupboard." He stares glumly at your golden chocolate bars and sighs. "I suppose ye can keep yer treasure, and you'd better 'ave these too." Captain Fluffy-Beard tosses a bunch of keys to Jimmy Smallhands. "I didn't really make the rest of yer crew walk the plank," he admits. "I locked 'em up in me ship's dungeon. Well, in *your* ship's dungeon."

Swashbucklin'!

You hoist the treasure chest onto your shoulder and Brenda helps you carry it back to the ship, where Jimmy Smallhands releases the rest of your crew from their cells.

"None of us will 'ave a rumbly tummy with so much chocolate to eat," smiles Jimmy, "and it's all thanks to you. Ye be the best crewmate we ever did 'ave."

"Yargh!" agrees One-Eyed Brenda.

"You've finished yer quest and you've taught them monkey-pirates a lesson they'll never forget. I don't reckon they'll be pilferin' our treasure again any time soon. Tell me, matey, did ye find the StoryQuest Star fer us too?"

If you were given a StoryQuest Star by Robinson Cuckoo, turn to the page number you saw glittering on it when he handed the item over.

If you don't have a StoryQuest Star, you've still finished your quest and you're still awesome! Turn to page 56.

"We're on a banana hunt," you tell Captain Fluffy-Beard. "Yep, we're just three banana-hunters and a rat out looking for some tasty yellow snacks. There are loads of them at the top of these two crossed-over trees, so if you don't mind, we'll just climb up and take a look."

The monkey-pirate captain narrows his eyes.

"Not so fast, landlubber," he says. "Oi'm a *monkey.* Don't ye reckon oi'd know if there were bananas on this island?" He has a point. "And if ye ain't 'ere for the fruit, oi reckons you've come to steal me chocolate coins. Well, the joke's on you, matey, because the treasure ain't hidden in this jungle, so you're lookin' in the wrong—"

Suddenly, a trapdoor is flung open under Captain Fluffy-Beard's feet. The tiny monkey shoots into the air like very small, very furry rocket and lands in a thorn-bush with his tail up over his head.

One-Eyed Brenda climbs out of the hole where the captain once stood.

"Brenda!" cries Jimmy Smallhands. "You're alive! Are ye all right, me hearty?"

Brenda points to the hole in the ground.

Jimmy gasps.

"Brenda says she's found a secret underground tunnel," explains the man. "She says she landed in it when the quicksand swallowed 'er up. She says she don't reckon the monkey-pirates know about it. She says it goes right across to the other side of the island."

Crikey, that One-Eyed Brenda is a real talker.

Captain Fluffy-Beard squirms inside the thorn-bush. He's so angry about having been fired across the jungle that his fur is standing on end. He looks like someone just took him out of the tumble-drier.

"We should scarper before Captain Fluffy-Beard gets outta that bush," says Jimmy Smallhands. "But these monkey-pirates be quick on their feet, matey. Oi'm worried he might catch up with us."

One-Eyed Brenda has an idea. She climbs back through the trapdoor and beckons you into the underground tunnel.

"Great idea, Brenda," you say. "Let's get out of here," and the three of you climb inside.

When the trapdoor closes, the passage is thrown into darkness. Brenda's eyeball lights up like a torch. It illuminates the tunnel and you follow the path all the way to the other side of the island, where you climb out through a second trapdoor.

There's an X on either side of you. One lies over the top of a small lagoon and the other has been formed by the broken mast of an ancient shipwreck. Which X would you like to investigate first, StoryQuester?

I'd like to go to the shipwreck please. Turn to page 82.

I'd rather go to the lagoon. Turn to page 53.

You jump down from the creeper and land in front of the little monkey ghost.

"I told you to get out of my ruin," snaps the ghost. "Right, that's it, prepare yourself for a woo-ing. *WOOO-OOOO-OOOO—*"

"Stop that right now!" you say, sternly. "It's really mean to frighten people. This ruin doesn't belong to you and if I want to search it, *I will*."

The monkey ghost's chin starts to wobble, she sniffs loudly and then a fountain of big, fat tears bursts out of her eyes.

"WAAAAAAAH!"

"Oh, no, please don't cry," you say, quickly. "I didn't mean to upset you."

"I thought frightening people was what ghosts are supposed to do," splutters the ghost. "What else can I do in this miserable old ruin?"

"Ye could play hide-and-seek," suggests Jimmy Smallhands, from up on the creeper.

The little monkey ghost's face lights up.

"I *love* hide-and-seek!" she smiles. "I'll count to twenty and you hide. Ready? Steady? Go! One, two, three, four…" and that's how you got stuck in an ancient ruin for a week playing hide-and-seek with a monkey ghost.

Go back to the start of the book to try again, or turn to page 32 to make a different choice.

The walls of the giant nostril are lined with moss. You take hold of the soft plant, pull yourself into the nose and climb until the glimmer of light turns into a gaping hole.

You can see the X on the top of Big Face Rock and…are those *feathers*?

Suddenly, the walls of the nostril start to tremble and a noise sounds from deep inside the rock.

AAAAAH…

It gets louder.

AAAAAAAAAH…

And louder.

AAAAAAAAAAAAAAH…

Until —

CHOOOOOOOOOOOOOOOO!

Big Face Rock sneezes you out of its nostril like a speck of dust. You fly across Monkey Island, over the ocean and all the way back to the mainland, where you land in the middle of a crazy golf course.

Your mum is standing there, tapping her watch.

"About time," she says. "Now, see if you can hit

that ball into the windmill."

Go back to the start of the book to try again, or turn to page 21 to make a different choice.

You take out the rat and throw it at the little monkey ghost. She catches the critter, smiles widely and strokes it like a cat.

"You brought me a hamster!" she cries. "I've always wanted a hamster, but Mummy wouldn't let me get one."

"That mangy varmint ain't no hamster," says Jimmy Smallhands, before you can stop him. "That's a—"

"Gerbil!" you cut in. "It's a gerbil. It hasn't got fleas, it doesn't bite and it definitely does *not* smell of wee. You can keep it, if you want."

The little monkey ghost kisses the stinky rodent on the end of its twitchy nose. The rat seems to like her too.

"It's the best present *ever*," she says. "You can take the treasure. I don't need it anymore. It's just me and my new pet from now on," and she disappears through one of the walls.

"Wait!" you cry. "What treasure?"

"Upstairs," calls the ghost, from beyond the brickwork. "Near the window…"

76

At that moment, a tiny shadow falls over the empty room. It's Captain Fluffy-Beard and he's not alone – *his entire crew are with him!*

"So, it looks like you've found me hidin' place," snarls the monkey-pirate leader. "Think yer gunna steal me chocolate coins, do ye? We'll soon see about that, matey."

Crikey, talk about out of the cannon and into the shark-infested waters! Will you make a dash for the treasure, or get the heck out of here?

I'll take my crew outside to safety. No amount of chocolate is worth getting hurt for. Turn to page 25.

I'll make a dash for the staircase and reach the treasure before Captain Fluffy-Beard knows what's happening. Turn to page 61.

You walk west until a crumbling ruin appears in the distance.

There's a rotten window-frame over the doorway. It forms a perfect X at the top of the building, so you step inside and head for a dusty staircase in the back wall.

Your footsteps echo through the empty chamber.

"See?" you say to your crewmates. "It's fine in here. There are no such things as—"

One-Eyed Brenda points a trembling finger over your shoulder.

"Y-y-yargh," she breathes.

You turn to find a pale figure floating behind you. She's a monkey, but she's not a pirate. She's white all over, completely see-through and she looks really grumpy. Yikes! It's a little monkey ghost!

"What're you doing in my ruin?" demands the little monkey ghost. "Get out of here before I scare you away with my ghostly woo-ing."

GULP.

You'd really like to leave now, but you'd also like to search upstairs for the treasure. What are you going to do?

I'll jump for one of the creepers and climb away. Turn to page 32.

Let's throw the rat at her. Turn to page 76.

You climb up to the crow's nest for a better look at the island. The view from here is fantastic. You can literally see right across to the other side of the—

SNAP!

Uh oh. The pole holding the crow's nest must have been damaged when the ship crashed and the extra weight has snapped it in two. You plummet towards the deck like a falling anchor, crash through the rotten wood and drop into the ship's galley.

You land next to a very hairy man.

He's carving a face into a coconut.

"How good of you to drop in on us," he says. "Oh dear, you seem to have hurt yourself. Have a drink out of Mr Coconut's head. It'll make you feel much better."

But drinking out of Mr Coconut's head doesn't make you feel better, so your crewmates wrap you up in bandages like an Egyptian mummy and send you back to the mainland to recover.

Go back to the start of the book to try again, or turn to page 54 to make a different choice.

You bite through the fishing-line and land on the grass at the side of the lagoon. Your crewmates take off like the wind, trying to escape the furry clutches of Big Baboon Bob.

But running is hard when you're dressed as a shark. You keep tripping over your tail and you can't see past your coconut teeth. Big Baboon Bob isn't the quickest monkey on the island, but he's catching up fast.

You'll need to think of a way to stop him, but how?

I'll ask Brenda to take out her telescopic eyeball and show it to Big Baboon Bob. That's enough to stop anyone in their tracks. Turn to page 5.
I'll shout, "Oh look, there's a bear!" and point over Big Baboon Bob's shoulder. Turn to page 60.

As you head towards the shipwreck on the eastern coast of the island, you pass a sign saying: WARNING – SHARK-INFESTED WATERS. It looks like you had a lucky escape when you avoided that lagoon, matey.

Swashbucklin'!

The land near the shipwreck is rocky and steep, and the huge wreckage of the old vessel looms on the coastline like the washed-up carcass of an ancient sea-monster. Two pieces of its great mast have snapped off and landed in an X shape on what's left of the decking. You'll need to take a closer look if you want to search for the treasure.

There are two ways to get up to the deck: you could climb the fallen rigging on the outside of the boat, or go in through a hole in its starboard side. Which would you like to do?

To climb the rigging on the outside of the shipwreck, turn to page 33.
To go through the hole and into the ship, turn to page 44.

You leave the water on the table and climb up a wooden flight of steps to the ship's deck. The old wreckage is creaky and damp, its sails are tattered and torn, the crow's nest has actual crows in it and the cannons are covered in barnacles.

You walk towards the broken mast to investigate the X. There's an old rum barrel directly below the cross, but you search inside it to find nothing more than seasnails and crabs. There's not a single chocolate coin on this whole bloomin' ship!

As you turn to leave, you see two identical monkey-pirates standing behind you. Eek! It's the Howler Twins! They're Captain Fluffy-Beard's first and second mates.

"What're ye doin' on our shipwreck, ye mangy varmint?" snarls the first twin.

"Yer a mangy varmint!" laughs the second. "Yo, ho, ho, ho, hooo!"

You try to think of a convincing answer, but instead you reply, "I'm delivering pizzas."

You're not sure why you said that.

"You can't deliver pizzas 'ere," says the first

Howler Twin. "It's only monkey-pirates what are allowed on Monkey Island, ye hornswagglin' barrel-bellied blighter."

"Yer a hornswagglin' barrel-bellied blighter!" laughs the second. "Yo, ho, ho, ho, hooo!"

"If ye ain't a monkey-pirate, you'll 'ave to walk the plank, ye filthy parrot-faced rapscallion."

"Yer a filthy parrot-faced rapscallion! Yo, ho, ho, ho, hooo!" The second twin lowers his furry eyebrows. "What's a pizza?"

How are you going to escape from the twins?

If you'd like to tell them you're a monkey-pirate,
turn to page 47.
If you want to walk the plank and swim back to
shore, turn to page 11.

You drop the rat and the little monkey ghost catches it. Her eyes sparkle as she strokes it like a cat.

"You brought me a hamster!" she cries. "I've always wanted a hamster, but my mummy wouldn't let me get one."

"That mangy varmint ain't no hamster," says Jimmy Smallhands, before you can stop him. "That's a—"

"Gerbil!" you cut in. "It's a gerbil. It hasn't got fleas, it doesn't bite and it definitely does *not* smell of wee. You can keep it, if you want."

The little monkey ghost kisses the stinky rodent on the end of its twitchy nose. The rat seems to like her too.

"It's the best present *ever!*" she cheers. "You can take the treasure. I don't need it anymore. It's just me and my new pet from now on," and she disappears through one of the walls.

"Wait!" you cry. "What treasure?"

"Upstairs," the ghost calls from beyond the brickwork. "Near the window…"

At that moment, a tiny shadow falls over the

empty room. It's Captain Fluffy-Beard and he's not alone – *his entire crew are with him!*

"So, it looks like you've found me hidin' place," snarls the monkey-pirate leader. "Think yer gunna steal me chocolate coins, do ye? We'll soon see about that, matey."

Crikey, talk about out of the cannon and into the shark-infested waters! Will you make a dash for the treasure, or get the heck out of here?

I'll take my crew outside to safety. Turn to page 25.

I'll make a dash for the staircase and reach the treasure before Captain Fluffy-Beard knows what's happening. Turn to page 30.

You march bravely onto the plank as if walking along a diving board at your local swimming pool and jump elegantly into the cool…

SPLODGE!

Oh, dear.

The tide is out at this time of day, so instead of landing in water, you've splatted into the muddy sand of the eastern coast. It takes five hours to dig yourself free, by which time the Howler Twins have captured your crewmates and eaten all of the chocolate coins for themselves.

Go back to the start of the book to try again, or turn to page 33 to make a different choice.

You run onto the quicksand to save One-Eyed Brenda, but the ground swallows you up like a tasty sandwich.

GULP!

You drop through the sand and find yourself in a secret underground tunnel. Brenda must have already wandered off and it's so dark down here you can't see where you're going, so you're forced to feel your way through the maze of passages.

It's three weeks before you find a way out. But you're an excellent friend for trying to rescue your crewmate, me hearty, so give yourself a piratey pat on the back then head to the mainland for a well-deserved rest.

Go back to the start of the book to try again, or turn to page 29 to make a different choice.

You climb down from the wreckage and onto the shore.

"Brenda," you say, "would you mind using your telescopic eyeball to search for another X?"

"Yargh!" replies One-Eyed Brenda.

A gentle whirring sound comes from inside the woman's head, as her eyeball spins in its socket.

WHIR! WHIR! WHIR! WHIR!

The pupil pops out like a tiny ice-cream cone.

POP!

And zooms in on the other side of the island with a rusty, *CREEEEEEEEAK!*

It's the most disgusting thing you've ever seen or heard in your life, but it's also pretty awesome.

Brenda points to the south of the island.

"She says there be another X on top o' Big Face Rock," explains Jimmy Smallhands. "But Big Face Rock is difficult to climb and dangerous too."

Brenda points to the west of the island.

"She also says there be an X in the window of an ancient ruin," says Jimmy, "but an evil spirit guards the buildin' and chases away anyone who goes near it.

I gotta tell ye, matey, I don't much fancy visitin' *either* place, but oi'll leave the choice up to ye."

Which X would you like to look at next?

An evil spirit? No, thanks! I'll go to Big Face Rock. Turn to page 31.
An evil spirit? Cool! I'll go to the ancient ruin. Turn to page 78.

Have you read the Christmas StoryQuest collection yet? Available now in paperback or eBook.

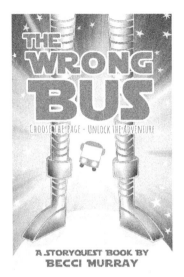

Can you navigate the endless universe in a bus…?

Or cure the Sheriff's horse of prickly fever in time for the rodeo?

STORYQUEST

CHOOSE THE PAGE - UNLOCK THE ADVENTURE

More books by the same author…

Laugh along with Billy, as he boosts his brain to the size of Venus in this hilariously gruesome chapter book also by Becci Murray.

Or try these very serious poems about really important stuff (like sausages, yaks and toenails) in this illustrated collection of rhyming silliness.

Becci Murray is a British author from Gloucestershire. She used to run a children's entertainment company, where she earned a living playing musical bumps and doing the Hokey Cokey (true story). Her favourite books are by Roald Dahl and she has a life-size BFG sticker on her bedroom wall (well, almost life-size).

You can learn more about Becci or send her a message by visiting the Llama House Children's Books website – she would love to hear from you!

www.llamahousebooks.com

Printed in Great Britain
by Amazon